Going to the Fair

Going to the Fair

written by
SHEREYL McFARLANE

illustrated by
SHEENA LOTT

EXHIBITION HALL

ORCA BOOK PUBLISHERS

ERIN'S eyes are as bright as the lights from the exhibition grounds and she can barely tear herself away from the window. The night lasts a thousand years. When she finally sleeps, Erin will dream first prize with a pumpkin grown to twice her size.

In the morning, excitement curbs her usual appetite. She grabs an apple and her bike. A bird on wheels, she's at the fair gates before her friends Kenji, Kate and Ben. As she waits impatiently, the road clogs up with cars and bikes and people. A chance for aunts and uncles to catch up on the family news. People laughing, neighbours chatting. Shouts of recognition from long-lost friends…

Inside the grounds a clown draws hoots of laughter when he shadows a young mother in the crowd, exaggerating her every move. She discovers his harmless prank and her laughter mingles with the crowd's.

Erin and her friends stop for cotton candy in pink and blue and green. Trading sticky strips of sweet spun sugar, they sprawl on bales of hay and listen to a barbershop quartet. The makeshift stage will offer up a steady stream of local talent throughout the day.

When Kate leaves to groom her calf, Ben drags the others to the antique machinery display. He helps his uncle fix up oldtime tractors on the weekends and knows them all: International Harvester, John Deere, Massey-Ferguson and Minneapolis-Moline — spit-shined until they gleam. His uncle lets them climb up into the seat of a perfectly restored vintage H. McCormick. Ben can hardly wait to drive it in the tractor parade the year he turns sixteen.

Nearby a group of farmers discuss the price of feeder hogs and this year's yield of hay.

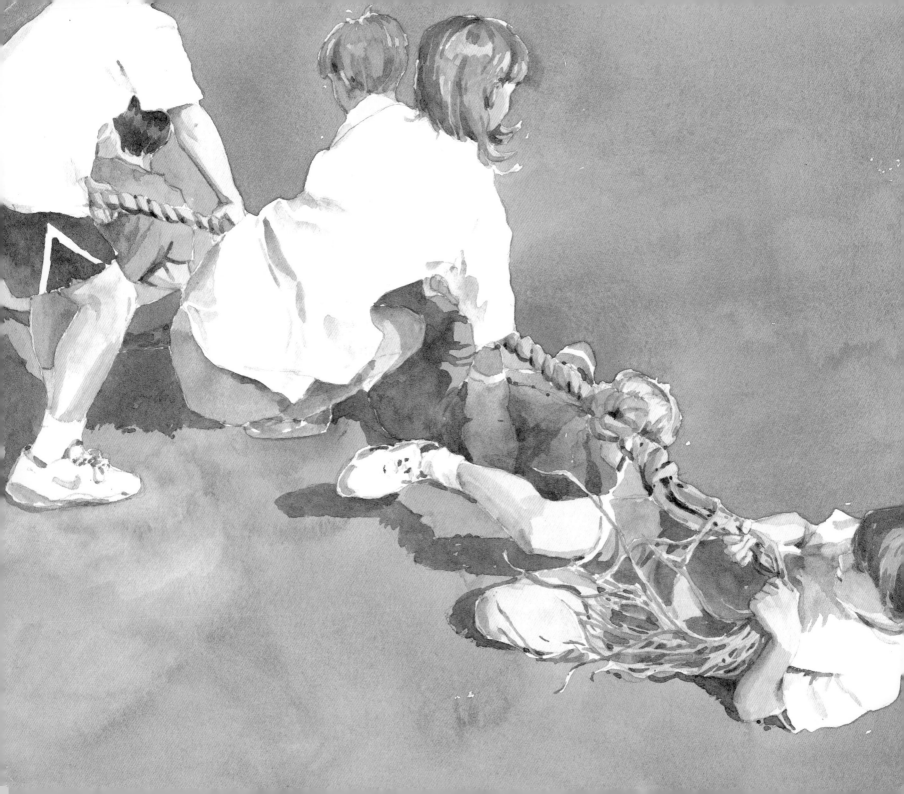

Bored with tractors, Erin tags along with Kenji. He has
promised to look after his little sister, Lena. Dragging her
brother by the hand, Lena leads the way to the tug-of-war.
But when the little girl spots the Pocket Lady, she drags
them off again. Kenji puts a quarter into her tiny, sticky
hand and she zigzags her way through the swarm of children
buzzing around the Pocket Lady like bees around a hive.
Lena reaches deep into an apron pocket for her prize. A
finger puppet? A clothes-peg doll? Squealing with delight,
she clutches a whirligig made by the church auxiliary.

Kenji is eager to show Erin his Barnavelder cock even though it didn't win a prize. The acrid smell of poultry hits them near the entrance of the tent. Kenji leads them down aisles of clucking, crowing, preening birds. Bearded, crested, long-tailed and silver-laced. Rows of Bantams, fancy Leghorns. Rhode Island Reds and Speckled Sussex hens, guinea fowl and geese. He lets them stroke his bird.

But Lena wrinkles up her nose. "Peeeewwh!" she protests. "Let's go. Let's go. Let's go!"

The 4-H Club is showing in the livestock ring. Kate is among the girls and boys leading calves past the scrutiny of judges. Points for strong and healthy heifers. Points for coats with a well-groomed sheen. Points for hindquarters straight and strong and clean.

Kate proudly leads her red-ribboned calf into the comfort of the livestock barn. It is dim and cool and pungent with the smell of manure and sweet hay. Past lines of stalls for cows and pigs and sheep. Her heifer stables near the only team of Clydesdales, but her grandpa says that the heavy horse teams numbered in the dozens in his day.

Erin and Kate meet at the food tent. Should they have burgers, dogs or chili? Buttered corn or giant dills? Root beer or lemonade? There are ice cream cones, blackberry scones and sweet cherry pie. It all smells so good. It's impossible to decide!

"How'd your pumpkin do?" Kate asks.

But Erin shrugs. She isn't sure that she really wants to know.

They pass Ben and Kenji cheering on contenders for the two-man crosscut saw. The six-foot blade glints like a mirror in the sun. A whistle blows and jagged teeth the size of fingers slip through wood like a knife through butter. Pull and push, heave and sweat. Their time looks good, but no one's touched the record yet.

"Let's go check," Kate insists, sucking on a honey stick.

Erin follows sluggishly. She's in no hurry to find out that she didn't win.

The walls of the exhibition hall are a kaleidoscope of quilts — Cherry Basket, Blazing Star and Tulip Appliqué. A great excuse for her to dawdle here and there along the way.

The aisle ahead is crammed with people. The garden club, no doubt. Some murmur praise, some disagree. Others nod their heads in sympathy. It seems that Miss Rubina's roses won first prize again this year. Poor Mr. T.! He works so hard! While Miss Rubina's flowers thrive upon neglect in her overgrown backyard.

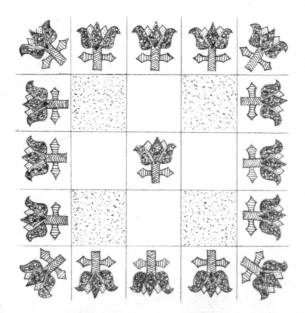

Weaving, sewing and crochet. Rows and rows of tables with this year's finest produce on display — potatoes and tomatoes, cauliflower, peas and beans. Parsnips, carrots, and several kinds of vegetables they've never even seen. Past peach preserves and pickled beets, jars of jelly and more of jam. Chocolate cake, butter tarts and raisin bread, cookies, pies and flan.

They pass zucchinis as long as baseball bats, cabbages the size of beach balls, some purple and some green.

Sunflower faces gaze serenely from the walls. "Maybe we should go?" Erin whispers. "I know I didn't win."

"A ribbon!" Kate shrieks excitedly.

Heads turn; some smile and others stare. But Erin and her friend are much too excited to even care.

"THIRD PRIZE!" They squeal and hug and dance toward the door.

The girls join Kenji and the others flinging hay in a haystack treasure hunt. Falling into a giggling heap, they suck their rock candy treats and fill each other in on the day. No one seems to mind that they look just like the scarecrows on display.

The crowds are thinning and the evening sun is sinking low.
Tired parents gather cranky children stubbornly insisting
that it's not yet time to go. Kenji and Lena wave goodbye.
Then Ben and Kate head off to meet her grandpa at the gate.

The exhibition lights are on when Erin drags her parents from the circle of gabbing grownups. She'll get her bike tomorrow when she and her dad pick up her pumpkin with the truck.

Before Erin snuggles into bed, she admires the ribbon pinned above her head. When she drifts off to sleep, giant pumpkin seed varieties will dance through her head — Prize Winner, Atlantic Giant and Ghost Rider. Aspen Spirit, Autumn Gold and Happy Jack — no matter, she's got a whole year to decide, the whole year ahead to dream first prize.

To all the participants and volunteers who make exhibition fairs a unique celebration of community.

S.M.

To Liz, Colby, Jennifer, Heather, Jessica, Matthew, Ben, Alex, Rachel, and all children who love to read.

S.L.

Text copyright © 1996 Sheryl McFarlane

Illustration copyright © 1996 Sheena Lott

Publication assistance provided by The Canada Council.

Orca Book Publishers
PO Box 5626, Stn B
Victoria, BC V8R 6S4
Canada

Orca Book Publishers
PO Box 468
Custer, WA 98240-0468
USA

Canadian Cataloguing in Publication Data

McFarlane, Sheryl, 1954 –

Going to the fair

ISBN 1-55143-062-2

I. Lott, Sheena, 1950 – II. Title.

PS8575.F39G64 1996   jC813'.54   C95-911165-4
PZ7.M48Go 1996

Printed and bound in Hong Kong.
Design by Christine Toller.

10 9 8 7 6 5 4 3 2 1